Copyright © 2023 by Nicole Heydenrijk. 845324

All rights reserved. No part of this book may be reproduced or transmitted in any form or by any means, electronic or mechanical, including photocopying, recording, or by any information storage and retrieval system, without permission in writing from the copyright owner.

This is a work of fiction. Names, characters, places and incidents either are the product of the author's imagination or are used fictitiously, and any resemblance to any actual persons, living or dead, events, or locales is entirely coincidental.

To order additional copies of this book, contact:
Xlibris
NZ TFN: 0800 008 756 (Toll Free inside the NZ)
NZ Local: 9-801 1905 (+64 9801 1905 from outside New Zealand)
www.xlibris.co.nz
Orders@ Xlibris.co.nz

Artwork, Text, Photographs © 2007
Nicole Heydenrijk and BodyFX NZ Ltd.

ISBN: 978-1-6698-8008-0 (sc)
ISBN: 978-1-6698-8009-7 (hc)
ISBN: 978-1-6698-8007-3 (e)

Library of Congress Control Number: 2022921613

Print information available on the last page

Rev. date: 07/26/2023

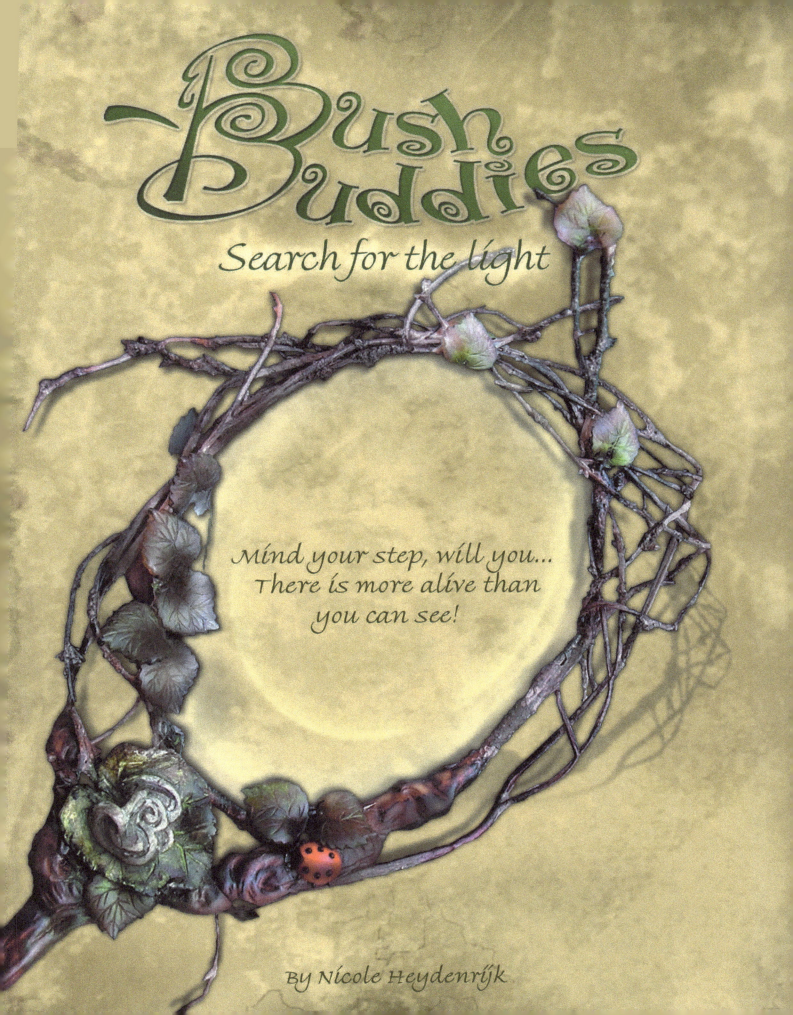

It is early morning in New Zealand. The Rimutaka Forest is sound asleep waiting for the first rays of sunlight. Dew drops drip from the long Toetoe grass. Everything is still and quiet, until...

"Yuck, that's wet!"

A small figure emerges from the grass. Grumpily ToiToi wipes the dew drops from his nose.

Suddenly a smile brightens up his face. He remembers his treasure. Excitedly he looks around and finds the little box in the long grass. He laughs happily as he picks it up and dances around with the box held high in his hands. Then he runs off.

Where is ToiToi going... and why is he so excited?

ToiToi is running to a place filled with lush green ferns. He starts searching in the bushes while shouting: "Fern, Fern wake up... where are you? Stop hiding Fern" From between the leaves a lovely little figure appears. It is Fern. She stretches and wipes her eyes. "Who says I'm hiding? I was still asleep. But, what are you doing up so early, ToiToi? What do you want? What time is it?"

ToiToi wants to show his treasure straight away but Fern needs to get ready first. She starts washing her face with dew that she collected from the Ferns. Then she arranges her leaves and sprinkles some water on her feet.
ToiToi gets impatient.
He holds the box right under her nose.
You have to guess what I found, yesterday evening.

Fern starts to laugh. Dear ToiToi. He always finds things and she knows he loves her magic. "All right, let me think." She lifts her hand in front of ToiToi's face. She closes her eyes slightly, peeking through her eyelashes to watch her friend. ToiToi keeps staring at her hand, he loves this game. Then Fern swiftly opens up her hand, while asking: "Is it a bird's nest?" Suddenly a bird's nest appears in her hand.
"No." says ToiToi, "Much smaller."
"What about a…..Fantail?" And a little bird pops up in her hand.
"No, it can't fly," says ToiToi.

ToiToi jumps from side to side excitedly.
He loves the way Fern can make things appear in the palm of her hand.
Patiently Fern tries again.
"Then maybe... it's a stick insect?" she suggests.
Looking closely at the insect, ToiToi shakes his head.
"No, no, no. It's not alive." he replies.
"What about a pinecone" Fern asks.
"Ha, wrong again. You'll never guess Fern."
ToiToi laughs and offers her the box.
"Here look for yourself."

Fern opens the box and looks inside. But she sees nothing.
Fern looks closely inside and outside the box.
"There is nothing here," she says.
ToiToi grabs the box from her. It is true. The box is completely empty.
He drops the box and sighs disappointedly: "It's gone!
You should have seen it Fern. It was so beautiful, a shining, little light.
I found it yesterday and put it in the box, to keep it safe."

Fern feels sorry for ToiToi and gives her little friend a big cuddle.

"Sorry you lost it ToiToi, but where did you find it?

Maybe we can get a new one?"

ToiToi shrugs. "It was so dark, I don't know if I can find the place again."

But they decide to try and hand in hand they start walking through the forest.

Soon they arrive at a clearing in the forest.
Before ToiToi can step into the open, Fern holds him back.
"We have to be careful ToiToi. There might be children out there."
ToiToi nods "When I hear something, I will hide straight away.
To be spotted by children or other humans is the worst thing
that can happen to Bushbuddies."
They walk carefully out into the open.
"Was it here somewhere?" asks Fern, looking around.
"No, there were a lot more bushes and trees."

They walk on until they reach a sandy path surrounded by
lots of bushes.
"Was it here then?" Fern asks.

But ToiToi shakes his head. "No Fern there was no sand, there was water!"
"Why didn't you say so? Come on lets go to the stream."
Fern starts running and soon they arrive at the stream.
Immediately Fern starts looking for the light. But ToiToi knows better.
"No Fern, this water is flat. My water was high with rocks all around. we won't find it here"

They follow the stream down through the forest, climbing over roots and crawling under the foliage.

Suddenly the ground moves and they hear an angry voice.
"Mind your step, will you. There is more alive than you can see."
Fern screams and immediately turns into a fern bush.
With one eye still open she whispers, "w-what was th-that?"
"Oh Fern, don't be silly. It's nothing to be scared of.
It's probably just another Bushbuddy, like us".

ToiToi looks down and starts talking to the ground.
"Hi, sorry we almost stepped on you. I'm ToiToi and this is Fern.
But who are you? And why are you hiding?" An ugly, earth creature looks
back and angrily rubs her arm. "I was hiding from you of course. You might
have been children. I couldn't know that, could I now. I can't see very well."
"But we are bush buddies too..." ToiToi laughs while Fern switches back
from a fern-bush. "Well I can see that, now." The Bushbuddy says looking
at ToiToi through a funny looking glass. "I am Muddum, the Bush buddy
of the earthworms.
But why on earth are you two stumbling around in the forest? You could be seen!"

13

"Oh no" says ToiToi proudly, "We are really careful."
Muddum rubs her sore arm "Yes of course you are.....I can still feel it."
ToiToi smiles a bit awkwardly at Muddum.

Then the old Bushbuddy asks, a bit more friendly, "Do you want to see something interesting? I know everything about the little wriggling creatures in the forest, and they all love me". Muddum settles within the leaves and starts cleaning her looking glass. Fern points at the looking glass and asks curiously "What is that?" Muddum holds her glass up high and replies:" This is my magical wormfinder. With this device I can find my worms even when they are underground. Let's see if I can find one to show you. "With her wormfinder close to her eyes she peers over the dirt and her huge body. "Oh yes here is Molly, oh you little rascal crawling back in the warmth again. Isn't she just adorable, with her little pink face?" Muddum smiles lovingly at the fat worm and asks inviting: " Do you want to hold her? Come sit beside me! I can tell you a lot about my little babies."

But ToiToi and Fern don't want to sit and play with worms. They want to go on with their search for the light. Maybe Muddum knows where to look?
"Of course I know" Muddum says thrilled, "In the sky!
A long time ago when I was still young and beautiful, I was always out in the open. I could see stars everywhere and I was one of them. A star amongst the stars."
When she thinks of the good old days Muddum gets very excited.
She rises out of the dirt; scattering worms and leaves everywhere, as she throws up her arms.

"I can still hear the sound of the applause, I was..."
Instantly Toi Toi looks up. Interrupting Muddum's memories, he shouts out loud.
"That's it... I remember the sound of running water!"
"A Waterfall" cries Fern excitedly.
"We have to listen for the sound of a waterfall!"
Muddum looks confused. "No" she says,
"It wasn't a waterfall, it was the trees applauding."

17

ToiToi and Fern are listening carefully for the sound of a waterfall, and pay no attention to the old bushbuddy. "Anyway, as I was saying", says Muddum, trying to keep their company a bit longer. "Why don't you just sit down? Then I can show you Molly. Now where has she gone?"

She looks down at herself to find the worm, but she can't find Molly, nor any of the other worms. "Oh my goodness!" she cries out loud. "Where have they all gone?"

In her excitement, Muddum has lost all the worms and now they're nowhere to be seen. Frantically she starts looking for them, calling their names. Meanwhile Toi Toi and Fern sneak away to continue their search for the light.

As they walk on, Fern and ToiToi are more careful. Bushbuddies could be hiding anywhere, in any bush or any shrub. ToiToi looks at the ground and watches where he puts his feet. Fern walks ahead and starts humming a song. ToiToi knows the song too and together they sing: "Now you see us... Now we're gone... That is how it's always done. Bushbuddies can be anywhere, Can't find them here, Can't find them there" ToiToi and Fern laugh and hand in hand they skip along the path Suddenly ToiToi stops, tilting his head as he listens carefully.

He starts jumping up and down and shouts, "Listen, do you hear it?"
Fern has heard the noise too and, following the stream, they run towards
the waterfall. Climbing over large rocks they find a lovely little spot
with dark rocks and water splashing down from above.

"This is the place," ToiToi calls out excitedly. They start looking everywhere; between the stones, in the soft moss and under the little fern leaves. But still they can't find the light. After a while ToiToi sits down on a rock, very sad and disappointed.

He was so sure he had found the spot where the light was.

"We'll never find it again, Fern", he sobs. "Never, ever!"

Suddenly they hear in a low voice "Maybe I can help?"

Fern jumps up and hides immediately, hissing: "Quick ToiToi, hide!"
But this time ToiToi doesn't need any encouragement and has already transformed into a Toetoe bush.
Who was that?

Slowly a figure appears among the rocks. He looks just like the rocks, but on his head is something that looks like an animal with lights and antenna's. Carefully ToiToi changes back into himself. "Don't be afraid," says the rock-creature friendly. "I am a Bushbuddy, just like you and my name is Rocko. But why are you here and what are you looking for?"

ToiToi explains to Rocko how he found a light yesterday, but then lost it.
"Do you know where we can find the light?" asks Fern.
Rocko starts to laugh, "Of course I do" he says warmly. "That's easy.
You only have to wait until dark. You can't see glow-worms during the day."
ToiToi and Fern look at each other confused. Rocko explains:
"That's what those lights are! Glow-worms! They are called worms but actually they are the tiny larvae of flies hanging from the rock-walls."
Rocko smiles and turns back to the wall, wiping the rocks very carefully.
"What are you doing, Rocko?" asks ToiToi.
"I am cleaning the rocks for the eggs that are ready to hatch.
I think it will happen tonight, so I have to be prepared."

ToiToi offers to help and Rocko asks him to move a large rock closer so he can clean it as well. ToiToi is eager to try and puts weight against the rock. The rock is very heavy and even with Fern's help; he can't move it a bit. "Sorry Rocko," he puffs "that rock is much too big for me to move. Nobody can move it."

"Never mind" says Rocko. "I'll do it myself."
He walks confidently towards the rock and lifts it with no difficulty at all.
After carrying it to the wall he places it down with ease.
Toi Toi gasps in awe," Wow, you are so strong Rocko!"
Rocko has to be strong to look after the glow-worms.
Because lots of glow-worms live in caves
Rocko often needs to move rocks to get near them.

"Are there many glow-worms, Rocko?" Fern asks curiously.
Rocko picks up a piece of bark and tries to count how many there are.
Maths is not his favourite subject and he keeps messing up
all his numbers. After a few attempts he hands
the bark to Fern, so she can figure it out!

Toi Toi is getting inpatient. Skipping little stones in the waterfall he asks, "When can we see the glow-worms?"
"You just have to wait till the sun goes down," says Rocko, looking back over his shoulder.
Soon it begins to darken and they all sit down on a large rock to wait. It doesn't take long before the first lights appear on the glistening wall.

"Look Toi Toi, there they are!" whispers Fern softly.
Holding their breath they watch as the whole wall begins to glow with little lights.
It feels as though they were standing on the edge of the world and the whole universe is right there in front of them.

"This is awesome," says ToiToi in amazement.
"I wish I could light up by myself."
"How do they do that Rocko?" Fern likes to know.
Rocko explains that they have a special liquid in their tail that lights up, to attract little flies and other tiny insects.

"They are like little fisherman," says Rocko. They catch their food with their sticky tentacles hanging down like fishing lines.
Wow, these guys are hungry. See? Their lights are very bright.
The brighter they glow, the hungrier they are. Sometimes, when there are not enough little insects around, I have to feed them."

There are more and more glowworms lighting up on the wall and Rocko starts running around feeding the little lights and helping the eggs to hatch.

ToiToi loves it. He is fascinated by Rocko's strength and light beams. He so wants to find his own magic. He knows that he will get it when he is older and wiser. But sometimes he just can't wait. He sighs deep. Then suddenly he gets a bright idea...

"Quick, Fern hand me the box. Now we can collect lots of lights." He jumps up and takes the box from Fern. But Rocko stops him. "If everyone took some glow-worms, soon they would all disappear. Then there'd be nothing left to enjoy. The glow-worms need to stay here, with me, in the forest, where it is dark and wet. Even if you only touch them, they will die."

ToiToi is very disappointed that he can't take the lights home with him.
But of course, Rocko is right and ToiToi is a little ashamed that he did take one home yesterday.
He didn't mean to hurt any glowworms.

"Feel free to hide here during the night," Rocko offers generously. "It is too dark to find your way home now." He turns and walks towards the rocks. Toi Toi elbows Fern in her side. "Wow, look Fern, he's got lights on his back too!" He says in amazement.

"Yes of course my back glows too" says Rocko "I belong with the glow-worms. I look after them and carry the weaker ones on my back to keep them close. I help all my glow-worms survive draughts and other dangers, like silly little Bushbuddies who want to collect them". He winks at ToiToi who tries to hide behind Fern. Rocko smiles. "Sorry, but I have work to do now. The eggs have to be planted on the new rocks and I need to count all the glow-worms to see if they are all there. So, good night. If you ever need me, you know where to find me."
As Rocko disappears ToiToi says in awe: "Wow, Rocko is so cool, looking after the glow-worms. And did you see how strong he is, Fern, moving that rock." Looking up at the moon he sighs: "I wish I was as strong. What will be my magic Fern?"
"I don't know ToiToi. First you have to do your great task, you know that, don't you?" asks Fern.

"Yes I do." ToiToi yawns. "But I am awfully tired now. Can we sleep here Fern? With the glow-worms?"
"I don't see why not," says Fern, looking around. "There's lots of cover and nobody will spot us here."
They both curl up together, and soon there are only a little fern and a Toetoe bush to be seen.
Fern sighs deeply: "They are just like stars... aren't they ToiToi?"

But ToiToi doesn't answer.
He is fast asleep, dreaming of new adventures.

More than just a book!

Bushbuddies is an interactive, hands-on project that teaches children and their parents about the New Zealand forest and nature in an innovative and fun way. In a time when there's more focus on environmental issues than ever before, Bushbuddies is an excellent way to introduce Kiwi children to ecology, conservation and the values that will protect our precious green New Zealand image.

Even though this book is created with The NZ nature and culture in mind, most topics are also relevant and interesting in other countries.

The programme also teaches children problem-solving, goal-setting and most of all how to have fun. Bushbuddies is a healthy mix of fact and fantasy with a case of humorous characters, designed to activate our children's love of nature.

With special thanks to the Actors:
Mike King, Alana Zivanovic, Andi Hulse, Matthew Pike

Bushbuddies is a production of
BodyFX New Zealand Ltd. Special FX studios

www.bodyfx.co.nz

Printed in the USA
CPSIA information can be obtained
at www.ICGtesting.com
LVHW071002150823
755285LV00010B/34